Table of Contents

HelloNeighbor™

The Neighbor's Notebook

The Official Guidebook

By Kiel Phegley

Scholastic Inc.

Photos ©: cover background: Hank Frentz/Shutterstock; cover pen: Rasdi Abdul Rahman/Shutterstock; cover parchment and throughout: nevermoregraphix/DeviantArt; back cover paper and throughout: Flas100/Shutterstock; back cover highlighter: Serg64/Shutterstock; 1 bottom paper and throughout: textures.com; 6 paperclip and throughout: AVS-Images/Shutterstock; 6 paper and throughout: Flas100/Shutterstock; 12 paper and throughout: Milos Luzanin/Shutterstock; 23 paper and throughout: textures. com; 24-25 folder and throughout: Mega Pixel/Shutterstock; 56 paper and throughout: R. Mackay Photography, LLC/Shutterstock; 70 cassettes: Senoldo/Shutterstock.

© tinyBuild, LLC. All Rights Reserved.
© 2019 DYNAMIC PIXELS™

All rights reserved. Published by Scholastic Inc., *Publishers since 1920*. SCHOLASTIC and associated logos are trademarks and/or registered trademarks of Scholastic Inc.

The publisher does not have any control over and does not assume any responsibility for author or third-party websites or their content.

No part of this publication may be reproduced, stored in a retrieval system, or transmitted in any form or by any means, electronic, mechanical, photocopying, recording, or otherwise, without written permission of the publisher. For information regarding permission, write to Scholastic Inc., Attention: Permissions Department, 557 Broadway, New York, NY 10012.

This book is a work of fiction. Names, characters, places, and incidents are either the product of the author's imagination or are used fictitiously, and any resemblance to actual persons, living or dead, business establishments, events, or locales is entirely coincidental.

ISBN 978-1-338-53762-8

10 9 8 7 6 5 4 3 2 1   19 20 21 22 23

Printed in the U.S.A.   40

First printing 2019

Book design by Cheung Tai

Raven Brooks Public Library

Librarian: Ms. Kyla Fleglie

"Hello, Neighbor!"

In your neighborhood, this may be an innocent greeting. Maybe you've heard Mrs. Brown say it as you walk to school, or Mr. Cruz shout it when you're walking your dog. But if you lived in Nicky Roth's part of town, those two simple words could turn, well . . . deadly.

You see, Nicky Roth's tale isn't exactly a happy one. Case studies rarely are, if we're being honest. But it is an interesting one—nay, a VERY interesting one. We don't always promise it'll be happy or joyous or wonderful or exuberant . . . but it will be eventful.

This compilation of careful research about Nicky Roth and the neighborhood he lived in is now available in one place, for the first time ever. Included, you'll find Nicky's own notes, newspaper clippings, and a whole lot more.

But don't say we didn't warn you.

CHAPTER 1:
Welcome to the Neighborhood

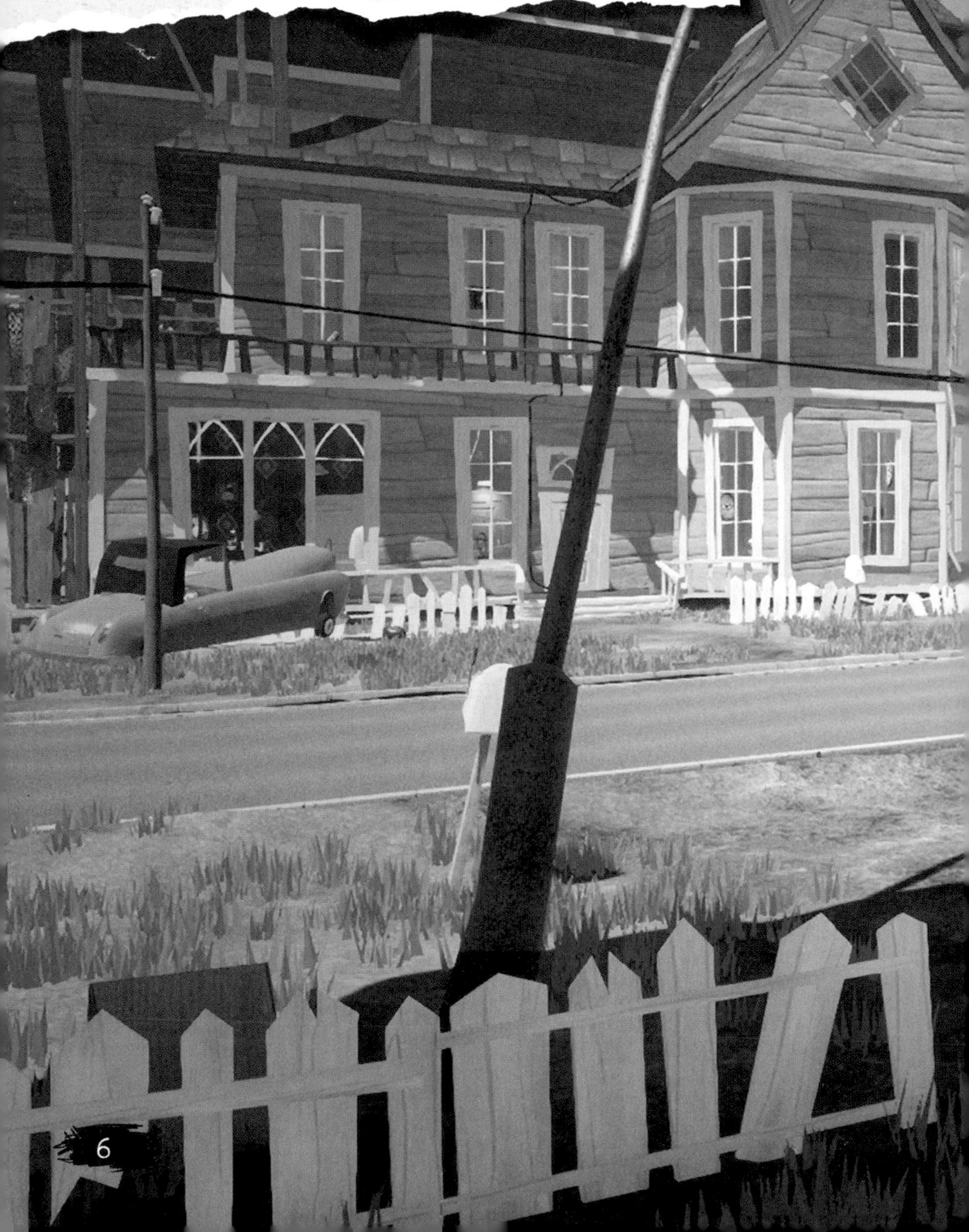

RAVEN BROOKS VOTED FOURTH-HAPPIEST TOWN IN THE DISTRICT

By Nala Sleuth / November 1995

It's official: Raven Brooks is the fourth-happiest town in the district!

Raven Brooks, with its gorgeous, luscious greenery, has officially been voted fourth-happiest town in the district.

The loosely populated town has long been known for its scenery. Local residents are now thrilled that it is gaining recognition for its happiness factor, too.

"When I heard the news, I couldn't help but smile from ear to ear," said long-term resident Greta von Beatrice-Gertrudo, seventy-five, of Raven Brooks. "We have a beautiful lake, a fantastic drainage system . . . and by golly, the neighborhood is pretty friendly, too!"

The town is also growing, and fast—the Roth family, for example, recently moved into a house on Friendly Court.

"We move around a lot because of our jobs, but we have never been more captivated by a town than Raven Brooks," said Jay Roth, thirty-six. "I look forward to creating many happy memories with my neighbors here."

Nicholas Michael Roth
AKA "Nicky"

"Let's go on an adventure into the deep unknown."

Nicky Roth! Such an inquisitive young soul. At times sarcastic, and ready for trouble. Always seen wearing his Sharkotron apparel, as well as his trusty neon-green watch and baseball cap. A great student.

— Mrs. Crawford

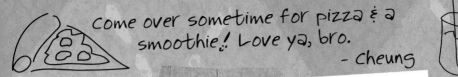

Come over sometime for pizza & a smoothie! Love ya, bro.
— Cheung

Name: Nicky Roth

Age: Twelve when the Roths moved to Raven Brooks in 1995

Siblings: Only child

Height: 4' 11"

Interests and Skills: Lockpicking, Engineering, Drawing, Inventing, Investigating, Adapting to new environments

Fears: Falling from heights, Supermarkets, Mannequins

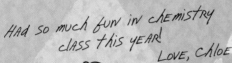

u rock, man. C ya next year.
— Enzo

HAd so much fun in chemistry class this YEAR!
LOVE, Chloe

Nicky! Thanks for saving my butt with math homework that one time. IOU major!
— HAGS!

NICKY NICK NICK—HAVE THE BEST VACATION EVER!

Most Likely To Get killed By His Creepy Neighbor! Hahaha, just kidding. Smell ya later!
— Maritza

Exploring a new hometown is always strange. Nicky Roth made a map of his new neighborhood upon moving in.

Golden Apple Candy Factory

Neighbor's house

Golden Apple Amusement Park

Opening Summer 1992!

Golden Apple Amusement Park

RAVEN ⊕ BROOKS ⊕ BANNER

DISGRACED ENGINEER QUITS, BLAMES ACCIDENT ON COMPANY

By Nala Sleuth

Local theme park designer, Theodore Masters Peterson, resigned from Golden Apple today. The infamous inventor denied all requests for interviews; however, he did release a statement.

"The rides I have designed meet all safety laws and precautions," the statement reads. "Any malfunction rests solely with the corporation who built and ran the attraction. I am truly sorry for anything the corporation has caused, but I repeat: My hands are clean."

Lawsuits are still pending on all sides of the tragedy, but for now, Peterson has retreated into his Raven Brooks home.

What is undeniable is that Golden Apple's "Rotten Core" roller coaster caused . . .

(Continued on 2A)

GOLDEN APPLE'S FUTURE UNCERTAIN

Raven Brooks's own candy company, Golden Apple, is on the brink of collapse following the Golden Apple Amusement Park tragedy. The office has been closed since Monday. Should collapse happen, hundreds of people appear likely to lose their jobs as a result.

Avoid At All Costs

The more Nicky learned about Mr. Peterson, the more it became clear to stay away. Due to our careful research, we've discovered some ways in which Nicky—or you, should you encounter Mr. Peterson for whatever unfortunate reason—could have avoided the Neighbor.

Noise Is Your Friend

* The best way to avoid the Neighbor is to distract him. Noisemakers like radios and alarm clocks are all over Raven Brooks, waiting to be set off and tossed away from you.

* Nothing gets a grown-up angrier than a good old-fashioned crank call. Inside Nicky's house, one could call Mr. Peterson to get him off the lawn.

Find a Place to Hide

* Being small is an advantage. If Mr. Peterson has you cornered, hide in a closet or cabinet to avoid capture.

* Once safe, spy on the Neighbor via the keyhole to know when the coast is clear.

When All Else Fails . . . Run!

* Mr. Peterson may be bigger, but Nicky is quicker. If he spots you, zip away and go home.

A Neighbor's Inventory

Around Raven Brooks, you'll see everything from ordinary junk to unfathomable inventions. But in order to survive, you'll need to be ready to turn anything into a weapon. Here are the items to watch for.

Moving Boxes & Trash Cans
These hefty neighborhood items are perfect for breaking windows, building ladders, and making mischief.

Lockpick & Keys
No one can pick a lock like Nicky Roth, but some doors in the Neighbor's house can't be opened without the right key. Never leave one behind.

Inventions
Nicky may not be designing deadly theme parks, but he has an inventor's eye. So items like the magnet gun and the key card-controlled electrical box are well within your control.

Tools

These common household items are worth more than you can imagine. In a tight spot, items like the wrench, the shovel, and the crowbar all help you break into and out of the Petersons'.

Golden Apple

This mysterious reward is more than a symbol of Raven Brooks's better days. Finding a Golden Apple is the only way you know you've truly mastered *Hello Neighbor*.

Masks

As you go beyond the original *Hello Neighbor*, you'll find wearing costumes is a perfect way to escape games like *Secret Neighbor* and *Hello Neighbor: Hide and Seek*.

Sonar

What Nicky wouldn't give to see the Neighbor coming through the walls! But at least his friends have an advantage with the sonar viewer found in *Secret Neighbor*.

Name: The Roth Family

Home: 909 Friendly Court

Current Status: Unknown

Nicky's family may have done him no favors by moving him to the house across the street from Mr. Peterson, but most of his Neighbor-fighting skills come from his mom and dad. Jay Roth was hired on as the editor of the *Raven Brooks Banner* in 1995, and aside from providing the archives that started Nicky's investigation, he also shared a sense of humor and of justice with his son.

Luanne Roth was a science wiz who took up a coveted research post at Raven Brooks University. From her, Nicky got his "cool under pressure" attitude, his inventive nature, and more than a little of his inquisitive, troublemaking outlook.

Friendly Court is anything but. The sun-drenched street where both Nicky Roth and Mr. Peterson once lived is the picture of suburban juxtaposition. On one side stood the Roth house: simple, orderly, and safe from prying eyes. This home can be relied on to stop the Neighbor from learning too much about how you move and play.

But of course, across the street was the real house of secrets. Mr. Peterson's house stood with its broken exterior and junk-strewn lawn.

Be it horrific or humble, there's no place like home. Enjoy yours while it lasts . . .

Name: Theodore Masters Peterson

Age: Forty when the Roths moved to the neighborhood

Height: 6' 4"

Interests and Skills: Designing "amusement" rides, engineering, inventing

Who is the Neighbor? Engineer or evildoer? Father or failure?

Whatever you label him, the man known as Mr. Peterson is a complicated threat. Despite how unhinged he may act whenever a passerby steps on his lawn, the Neighbor is a genius in his own right.

Unfortunately, the innovations in roller-coaster design that brought him fame also proved his undoing. Some would say he became more obsessed with breaking the laws of physics than with protecting and honoring life.

Nicky Roth discovered more than he bargained for when he met Mr. Peterson. But as you continue to dig through this study, remember that no matter how sad this man's story may seem, the real tragedy is how it turned him into a monster.

If his strong-man mustache and bulging biceps didn't already tell you, Mr. Peterson's grasp can't be broken. And while he'll tell people that his black gloves are for metalworking, Nicky knows that they also conceal his fingerprints when he puts you in a stranglehold.

WHAT BROKE MR. PETERSON?
by Nicky Roth

This is the question that has haunted me since the day we moved to Friendly Court.

At first, things seemed good. Raven Brooks was going to be my city, you know? I wasn't going to let any opportunity go to waste. He might have been strange, but the kid across the street wanted to be friends. His dad had lost it somewhere along the line, but whose pops hadn't?

Still, I wondered about his dad—Mr. Peterson—a lot. He wasn't kooky like my dad was—whereas my dad would haphazardly leave his coffee cup on the porch, Mr. Peterson, well ... would do a whole lot worse.

Was it Mr. Peterson's failed career that made him snap? I mean, long before the tragedy at the Golden Apple theme park (that no one in town seemed to talk about), the engineer's designs had been "scrutinized," or so my dad says.

Certainly, the auto accident he was involved in was a point of no return. But while he experienced great loss in a car crash, I was pretty sure he'd gone over the edge well before that. In fact, Mr. Peterson might have even had something to do with the crash.

And that made me think. What if the force driving Mr. Peterson's rage goes beyond human understanding? What if something far more sinister is at play? On the edges of night in Raven Brooks, some say a deadly and thorny Thing drives townspeople mad. And I've started to see it ... beyond the local gossip, anyway.

Name: Aaron Victor Peterson

Age: Twelve when things went wrong for his family

Height: 5' 1"

Interests and Skills: Lockpicking, terrorizing his little sister, taking things apart

When Nicky moved to town, Aaron Peterson became his best friend. The boys both loved lockpicking and trouble-making. Aaron's humor was a little dark—some would even say his picking on his sister was a bit pathological, or that his mood was secretive and somber—but he still proved a good friend.

Yet even as Aaron withdrew from his life, Nicky knew he couldn't give up his investigation into Mr. Peterson, especially not if there was a chance Aaron was in trouble.

But with bad omens everywhere, was Aaron a victim . . . or perhaps another kind of strange villain in this saga?

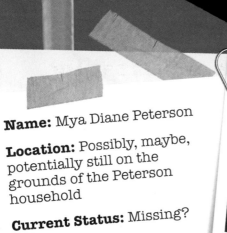

Name: Mya Diane Peterson

Location: Possibly, maybe, potentially still on the grounds of the Peterson household

Current Status: Missing?

At ten years old, Mya Peterson was a ray of sunshine in a gloomy household. She was bright, funny, and ready to investigate the world. But as Nicky Roth found out too late, Mya was standing too close to the incident at Golden Apple Amusement Park. Since then, she walked through the world with a certain kind of sadness. And it didn't help that her father and brother both seemed to be preparing her for some bizarre survival training.

Where was Mya when Nicky started his quest to unlock the secrets within the Peterson house? Hopefully alive and well.

Of course, there's no hiding what happened to Mrs. Peterson, even as her husband tried to erase the memory of his dearly departed wife.

A *Hello Neighbor* Timeline

The story of what happens between Nicky, the Petersons, and the town of Raven Brooks can be experienced on and off the screen. And while this notebook covers the major twists of the entire series, there's nothing better than experiencing the terror of the Neighbor firsthand. Here's the chronology of everything *Hello Neighbor*.

The story of Nicky's move and his friendship with Aaron start you on the dark path.

Experience Aaron's and Mya's lives after their tragic loss with this shocking DLC prequel.

The final fate of the Petersons revealed!

Nicky's original adventure into the dark secrets of Mr. Peterson's world remains the heart of the series . . .

. . . but don't miss *Secret Neighbor*, the new multiplayer hit that takes place during the action of the original *Hello Neighbor*!

CHAPTER 2:

Discovering the Missing Pieces

Raven Brooks Public Library

Librarian: Ms. Kyla Fleglie

Nicky Roth was (as many people were) exceptionally curious about the Peterson house and the family that lived inside it. That curiosity was made even curiouser when Aaron Peterson invited Nicky over and the two developed a companionship.

In this section of our study, you'll find many documents that Nicky kept, as well as his own personal recordings. Maybe you too will be able to get a picture of what happened in Raven Brooks.

RAVEN ⊕ BROOKS ⊕ BANNER

Local Engineer Brings World-Renowned Talent Home

PETERSON HAS DESIGNED PARKS ON SIX CONTINENTS! READ ON FOR A SNEAK PEEK OF HIS LATEST UNDERTAKING!

Residents of Raven Brooks, meet local Engineer Theodore Masters Peterson.

Although Mr. Peterson may look like the common suburban father, he's also the ingenious engineer behind the soon-to-be-opened Golden Apple Amusement Park.

Golden Apple Amusement Park, from its Honey Crisp Carousel to the Evil Orchard maze, was completely designed within the walls of Mr. Peterson's Friendly Court home in Raven Brooks.

So, what's the method behind the madness?

"I like to keep my working methods a secret," said Mr. Peterson, thirty-seven. "But I can ensure people that the rides at Golden Apple will be some of the fastest, scariest attractions in the country."

Peterson holds multiple degrees in engineering and physics. This gives his rides somewhat of a gravity-defying grace.

The park, which opens next week, is projected to have an unprecedented opening-day crowd. Which left us wondering . . . what does Mr. Peterson has up his sleeve? Any secrets or surprises?

"You'll just have to wait and see," Mr. Peterson teased. "I'll give you a hint, though. Have you noticed there's no roller coaster in this park?"

Raven Brooks Youth Mya Peterson Start Young Inventors Club *(See A4)*

RAVEN ⊕ BROOKS ⊕ BANNER

Golden Apple Amusement Park Burns to the Ground

INVESTIGATION CONTINUES* PETERSON'S PAST RESURFACES* YI FAMILY DEMANDS ANSWERS

Following the tragic death of seven-year-old Lucy Yi at Golden Apple Amusement Park, law enforcement is demanding to know why a dangerous roller coaster was allowed to operate before passing certain critical inspections.

My dad says the most important part of investigating is recording information. He always has a notebook filled with information about what he sees. My baby book is full of that weird stuff. See what I mean?

TODAY, NICHOLAS IS THIRTEEN MONTHS OLD.

HE CAN SAY: MAMA, DADA, ME

HE LIKES: LOOKING OUT THE WINDOW, JUMPING UP AND DOWN (EVEN WHEN SITTING!)

FAVORITE FOOD: MUSHY PEAS

And while I wish my dad wouldn't constantly remind me that I used to love peas (ugh, I really hate peas), I like knowing things about what happened or what's going on.

Aaron has invited me over to his house a few times, so I've been able to get the gist of what the Peterson household is like.

THE PETERSON HOUSE: WHAT'S INSIDE

The first rooms have all the things you'd expect: couches, TVs, and tables. But there's a layer of dust on everything, and random junk like bowling balls and moving boxes clutter up the place.

Aaron took me upstairs to his room, but I can't remember how we got there. Most rooms are locked up tight, and I think the walls may be moving. Every time I come back, doors and hallways seem to have shifted. And if I ever walk toward an "unapproved" area, Mr. P is right there to push me away.

There's a big lock on the basement door. Aaron says that the basement is his dad's workshop, but something doesn't feel right to me. It feels like the only way I can really figure out what's going on . . . is to break a few windows.

BREAK A FEW WINDOWS

To enter the basement, you'll need to break some windows. To do so, you should smash them with something ideally heavy. However, if you want to avoid being caught, you'll need to perform a variety of techniques to outsmart Mr. Peterson. Here are two tried-and-true ideas that you can use!

- Ding Dong Ditch—Ring the Neighbor's doorbell, then run around and sneak your way in.

- Naptime—Take some sleeping pills from the cabinet in the bathroom and put them in a fresh glass of milk. When the Neighbor drinks it, he'll fall asleep. (Just remember, like all this stuff, NEVER do this to anyone but the Neighbor!)

COME VISIT
GOLDEN APPLE CANDY FACTORY!

It's the most golden place in Raven Brooks!
Packages begin at only $39.99 a person
Open seven days a week!

Attractions Include:

- Live entertainment!
- Caramel-Pulling Contest
- The soon-to-be world-famous Sugar Shack
- Candy jugglers
- Costumed sweet meet-and-greets
- Games!
- Sour Apple Endurance Test—how many can YOU eat?
- Put your skills to the test with the Candy Wrapper Wrap-Up Game!
- Toss-a-Pop—Toss lollipops and other candies onto the Golden Apple Tree and win prizes!
- Dining!
- CANDY, CANDY, CANDY—Oh, and did we mention candy?
- Sour Gummy Restaurant—Where everything is sour!
- The Golden Experience—Reservations must be made in advance to unlock the Golden Experience experience. Includes dishes prepared with 24K gold.
- Rot Your Teeth—A whole new dining experience, complete with toothbrushes at the end! Have questions? Make a reservation now . . .
- Rides!
- The best rides in all Raven Brooks—Nay, the world! So great you'll have to come check them out yourself. The surprise is worth the (long line) wait!

RE: Ongoing "CODE SILVER PEAR" Investigation
From: Hannah Bull <hannah.bull@ravenbrookspolice.com>
To: Marcus Redfin <marcus.redfin@ravenbrookspolice.com>

The Golden Apple Corporation has found a history of disturbing "accidents" that share one common factor: They were designed by Theodore Masters Peterson.

Unfortunately, I no longer believe these are "accidents."

Mr. Peterson possesses no certification in safety, nor has he ever taken a reputable safety procedure course.

Mr. Peterson has never donated blood, never taken a CPR lesson, never volunteered at his children's school, and failed his driver's license six times in New Jersey, New York, California, Delaware, Connecticut, and North Carolina before finally passing in the state of Florida.

Over the course of his life, Mr. Peterson has accrued twenty-nine parking tickets, sixteen speeding tickets, and most notably, two seat-belt safety tickets.

Mr. Peterson is banned from entering Toys & Burritos, the half-toy store, half-Mexican cuisine retail-restaurant where his daughter had her sixth birthday party, due to a "behavioral incident."

It is my unfortunate conclusion that Mr. Peterson seems to not understand or simply not care about core safety.

In secrecy,
Hannah Bull
Investigator
Raven Brooks Police Department

Traffic Citation

Revised 01/89

☐ D.L #		
☐ COM DL#		
☐ I.D #		

Ticket Number

02241993

D.L State	D.L Type: A B C M

LAST NAME PETERSON **FIRST NAME** THEODORE

RESIDENCE ADDRESS 910 FRIENDLY COURT

STATE	ZIP CODE		CITY
		RES PHONE	

SOCIAL SECURITY NUMBER

WHITE   BLACK   HISPANIC
ASIAN   OTHER

CITY	DATE OF BIRTH

EMPLOYER

BUSINESS PHONE

SEX	HEIGHT	EYES

BUSINESS ADDRESS

VEH COLOR	VEH YEAR	VECHICLE MAKE	BODY TYPE	REGISTRATION	STATE	LICENSE PLATE #

VIOLATION DATE	TIME	CONDITION	MUNICIPAL COURT use only

VIOLATION LOCATION
CORNER OF LEVI AVE + RENSOP STREET

COUNTY   DIRECTION

VIOLATION (A) DRIVING 30 miles ABOVE the SPEED limit

VIOLATION (B)

Next up on my investigation list: Golden Apple Amusement Park.

I'm sure if I'd lived in Raven Brooks when this was being built, I would have been excited. But it's been a few years now since it's been closed.

That doesn't stop the Peterson kids from going back, though—Mya in particular. So I've traipsed around the Golden Apple Amusement Park, and I'll sum it up best in one word: "yeesh."

Yeeshes aside, this place is UNRULY. And dirty. But that doesn't stop Mya from going back, again and again.

I guess the amusement park is the place where Mya feels most comfortable. She must have gotten her dad's gift for invention because she's the only person able to rev up attractions like the carousel, and she generally knows the ins and outs of every part of the park.

Mya's tried to explain to me what's really going on under the surface, but she seems afraid to say out loud whatever is really going on in that house.

Weird, right?

Local Mother Dies in Tragic Accident

By Nala Sleuth

Diane Peterson died this week in what police are calling an unexplained car collision. The teacher and mother of two was found nonresponsive when police arrived on the scene.

Her husband, Theodore Masters Peterson, was driving the car. He also made the phone call to authorities to come rescue his wife. Police believe he may have fallen asleep at the wheel.

The Peterson family has been in the news of late as the victim's husband has been blamed by many for the accident that claimed the life of seven-year-old Lucy Yi at the now-shuttered Golden Apple Amusement Park.

(Continued on A2)

Peterson Not Charged in Death of Lucy Yi

A sad chapter in the history of Raven Brooks has come to a close, and many are speaking out against the state as a result.

While the court of public opinion has already judged engineer Theodore Masters Peterson harshly for the part he played in the creation of the faulty Rotten Core roller coaster, a State court ruling found that sole responsibility for the death of Lucy Yi rested with the Golden Apple Corporation, who owned and operated the site.

However, the hard facts of the case provided few conclusive answers. Young Ms. Yi lost her life when the cars of the Rotten Core ride careened out of control, but investigators could not determine whether an electrical malfunction or a base structural design flaw caused the crash. And when the remains of the roller coaster burned to the ground in a fit of mob outrage at the site, all other evidence was lost.

At only seven years old, Lucy Yi had made her mark on the town for her innovative co-founding of the Golden Apple Young Inventors Club and was beloved by classmates and school teachers as a bright, cheerful presence.

So Lucy and Mya
were part of the
same club. Hmm.

CHAPTER 3:
Hide and Seek!

Raven Brooks Public Library

Librarian: Ms. Kyla Fleglie

In the DLC prequel game *Hello Neighbor: Hide and Seek*, you'll see the world through the eyes of ten-year-old Mya, three years after the death of her friend Lucy.

When we join Mya, life in the Peterson household seems loving and stable. She and her brother, Aaron, love to play games with each other, which you will join in on.

What's more, *Hide and Seek* takes place around the same time that Nicky moved in across the street. You can spot him by looking out any upstairs window that faces his home.

My lil sis-iah, Pariah Mya—
I hope you don't mind me slipping
this note underneath your door.
Do you want to play a game?
This one's all about animals!
It's going to be tons of fun.
It's called Savanna!

Level 1:
The Wild

Your first challenge as Mya is to play explorer in the make-believe Savanna. It's your job to gather sixteen stuffed animals and return them to the basket before you're caught by your brother. There are a few corners and holes to hide in should you need to.

Those animals can be obtained here:

- Lion—Under an arch made of rocks on the first level. To coax the lion out of its cave, you'll need to pick up a steak that's hidden underwater, then drop it in front of the lion. You can collect the lion when it comes out to eat.

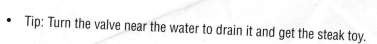

- Tip: Turn the valve near the water to drain it and get the steak toy.

- Bird—Jump or use the gust of a geyser to access the wardrobe and obtain a weapon. Then proceed to the upper level. Once there, collect the egg that's in the nest—this will trigger a large bird that will drop a toy. (Get out of the bird's way—if it gets you, you'll be forced to restart.) Next, collect the bird toy by attacking it with your weapon.

- Monkey—Use your weapon at a large tree and shoot down the monkey, then collect it.

- Rhinoceroses—There are two rhinoceroses to collect. The first one is on a shelf. Obtain it by using the air flow from a geyser. Then jump down to the lower shelf and collect the second one on a drawer.

- Goat—Find the goat on top of a mountain of boxes. You can get there by climbing the boxes or using a geyser.

- Zebras—You'll collect two zebras in the game. The first is on the table next to the lemur. The second is in a bucket. You'll need to use the airflow from a geyser to jump to it.

- Mole—Throughout the map, collect boxes. You'll need them to repair the holes that the mole creates. When you're done, you'll find the mole in the last uncovered hole.

- Bear—Located under a bird-chair toy. This toy makes a lot of noise when you get near it. Create a distraction so that you can distract your brother—try the basketball!

- Lemurs—There are four lemur toys you'll need to collect. You can find them:

  - Next to a big brush

  - On a drawer (Hint: Use a geyser to get up)

  - On the couch

  - On the table next to the zebra

- Elephants—There are two elephants in the game. The first is hanging from a painting on the wall—you'll want to use the gust of a geyser to reach it. The second elephant is on top of a drawer. You'll also need to use a geyser to get this one.

After the first level, we check in on the Petersons at the family dinner table. While mom is still in the mix, Aaron treats Mya kindly by sharing the big soup spoon with his sister.

CASH RECEIPT
*****

RAVEN BROOKS GROCERY MARKET
So fresh . . . it's great!
ROUTE 1
*****

| Manager: | Pepper Lotz |
| Cashier: | Michael Smith |

= == == == == == == == == == == == =

Bananas .95 EA/	
Coconut oil	0.95
hard salami	1.99
Turkey breast	3.98
Chocolate frosting	6.99
	1.00

- -- -- -- -- -- -- -- -- -- -- -- --

Tax 6%	
Total	0.89
CASH TEND	15.80
CHANGE DUE	20.00
	4.20

- -- -- -- -- -- -- -- -- -- -- -- --

ITEMS SOLD 5
#Transaction 16AGDF46646D44

THANK YOU

Peterson Family Secret Soup Recipe

- 2 handfuls of spinach
- 1.5 cups of water
- 1 tbsp of coconut oil
- 2 cloves of garlic
- 1 carrot
- 1 onion
- 3 cups of bone broth
- 1 cup of cashews

Level 2:
Policeman and Bank Robber

In the next game, Aaron is a police officer and Mya is a bank robber, looking for sacks of cash. You'll need to collect all thirty-three bags of money in this level. However, if you leave a bag behind, it'll spawn in a random place—so don't do that!

Where to search:

- Take a look under benches—there are some bags hiding under there.

- Inside safes. The code you'll need to use is 137.

- On the roof. Get on the roof by causing a distraction, then quickly run under the car to the nearest building and use boards and doors to climb to the roof. Make your way to the next roof (Tip: Use the chimney). Access the next building by using a rope. Once there, you'll spot two bags of money as well as a special golden key. Return to the room by jumping on the trampoline. Speaking of which . . . you'll find some money in the picture on the wall!

- Check the trunks of broken cars.

- Sift through shelves and desks.

Level 3:
Firefighting Family

Things get interesting in the third level. The Peterson parents are missing. Aaron decides to distract Mya with a new game— she must collect dolls from around the house and save them from a fire.

Where to search:

- Enter the level by using the oven mitt on the top bunk of the bed in the kids' room.

- Items are key. Start by getting the silver food lid off the dining room table (you'll also find a doll underneath).

- Use the silver food lid to put out the fire by the blue squirt gun. Then collect it for later use.

- Fill the squirt gun with water from the old bathtub, then scale the building directly across from the big turquoise clock. Inside its upper floors, you will find a burning gas pipe. Put the flames out with your squirt gun, and turn the pipe's handle with your oven mitt. This will release a stream of gas on the rooftop.

- Ride the rooftop gas up into the sky and make your landing in the room full of mattresses. Add one mattress to your inventory and place it outside a burning building for it to capture four dolls jumping to safety.

- In the most challenging rescue mission of this level, you'll need to douse the whole map in water. Head to the outskirts where you can turn a lever that gets the water pumping. Then jump off the cloud to both reach the final rooftop and let the rain fall.

- The last dolls in this level can be spotted by the Christmas tree they gather around.

kids, I have something
~~important to~~
~~Something's happened~~
~~This is not good news~~

kids—your mother ~~died~~ is
gone.

Hide and Seek is more than a game of cat-and-mouse for Mya and Aaron. This is also the game where we see most closely the impact Mr. Peterson has on his children. And it all starts with the deadly crash.

As the game goes on, Mr. Peterson continues to come down on his kids hard, Aaron most of all.

That's because Mr. Peterson considers his son to be the source of his problems. He thinks Aaron is a "bad omen"—the reason why his countless theme parks have imploded.

Level 4:
The Zombie Graveyard

In the wake of their mother's death, Aaron Peterson took his anger over the edge. When Mya attempts to reach out to her brother, Aaron turns from angry tears to a dangerous new game involving a shotgun. That leads us directly into the Zombie Graveyard level—one of the most harrowing of the entire game where Mya needs to track down *braaaaaaiiiiiins* or risk never returning to a normal life.

- Start by heading to the shack with a bearskin rug on the floor. Upstairs is a lever next to the number 13. Turn it and make sure to grab the book sitting on the lectern as well.

- Next you'll want to turn some levers out in the yard. On the far side is another 13 marking your second lever, and then 25 is tucked away near the structure built on pipes. These will grant you access to two key items: the crowbar that's near the frozen lake and the shovel, which sits at the bottom of the bell tower.

- Use the crowbar to pry the boards off the front of the abandoned meat market, and in there you will discover a cache of brains. The shovel allows you to dig into black dirt and any point in the level and your grave-robbing will reward you with more brains for the basket.

- A harder-to-find brain awaits you in the room with the busted TV. Smash that TV with your crowbar and set the book on the table to unlock a brain resting above the chair.

- The last major brain location is in the small building "guarded" by a handful of zombie figures. Bust your way through using your items and gather your final bits of gray matter in order to bury this level completely.

CHAPTER 4:
Nicky's Waking Nightmare

In the *Hello Neighbor* novel *Waking Nightmare*, readers discover that Aaron and Mya have disappeared. Prophetic dreams haunt Nicky every night. Mr. Peterson grows angry and his behavior becomes more erratic. And for the first time, strange creatures seem to rise from the ashes of the Golden Apple tragedy.

N—
THE SCHOOL COUNSELOR
THINKS IT'LL HELP YOUR
BAD DREAMS GO AWAY IF
YOU WRITE THEM DOWN.
YOU CAN USE THIS BOOK. I
LOVE YOU.

　　　　　　　　　— MOM

January 13, 1996

Woke up in a sweat. Dreamt I cracked open a bank vault.

January 13, 1996

Woke up again. This time I dreamt I crashed into a wall.

January 14, 1996

Didn't sleep much after that. Everyone is tired of me falling asleep in weird places— like school or when Mom drives me to school. I had another dream last night where skeletal hands reached out, ready to pull me into the murky void.

January 15, 1996

The school counselor says I need to write down everything I dream about, so, well, here's everything.

I dream about the Petersons a lot. Last night, I dreamt that I was back at Golden Apple Amusement Park with Aaron. We were out doing the usual: practicing lockpicking and making mischief! But then I'd look around and . . . Aaron was GONE! In the dark, strange, scratching sounds chased after me . . . and then I woke up.

January 16, 1996

This was definitely my worst dream...
EVER.

I was at Golden Apple, and I was just
strapped into the Rotten Core coaster.
I was really excited, but then BAM! It
rattled and I rushed around in dizzying
circles. My fellow riders were screaming. I
was screaming, too. I could hear the sound
of iron bars buckling under pressure and the
hot hiss of breaks burning out. And just as it
seemed cart would lift off the track and
hurtle me to the ground... I woke up.

Sometimes I wonder. Are my dreams
someone else's memories? Or maybe I'm...
seeing into the future?

I'm taking Dad's advice again and writing down everything I see. Aaron and Mya are missing. Mr. Peterson's convinced the whole town that they went to live someplace else, but I don't buy that. For MANY REASONS. Wouldn't they at least send a postcard?

Took this picture almost four months ago from across the street. It was only the week after we lost Mrs. P. Mr. P only takes the car by himself for joyrides. No movers ever showed up to get Aaron's and Mya's stuff.

Aunt Lisa
555-0127

Mr. Peterson told everyone that Aaron and Mya are staying with his sister, Lisa, but the woman at this number denied it and hung up.

Raven Brooks Middle School

Dear Nicholas,

We understand you were neighbors with Aaron Peterson before he was pulled from school. While his father has filed paperwork for his transfer, we haven't been able to transmit them to his new instution. We'd love for Aaron to have a record of the work he's completed at Raven Brooks Middle. Could you drop this off with Mr. Peterson?

Thank you,
- Mrs. King

I left that packet on the Petersons' porch and watched Mr. P. crumple it into a ball from my room. No one believes me, though—of course.

Found this bracelet outside my house. Mya must have left it behind. But here's the real question: Was it hers, or did it belong to Lucy Yi? And more importantly, is this all that's left of them?

GOLDEN APPLE
YOUNG INVENTORS
CLUB

Raven Brooks Public Library

Librarian: Ms. Kyla Fleglie

How exactly did Mr. Peterson tell a whole town that he'd shipped his kids off to another state? More important, how did they believe him? Well, a huge part of it was putting on a normal front for the neighborhood.

Innocent people have nothing to hide, or so the theory goes. Following his children's disappearance, the Neighbor wandered around his property, taking out the trash and surveying his lawn—just like any other suburban dad.

But Nicky Roth couldn't be fooled. He had seen firsthand the way Mr. Peterson could transform from doting father to raging beast.

In order to prove his suspicions, Nicky began a spying campaign that tracked Mr. Peterson day and night. He snuck around the Peterson house, rummaging through the trash and even secretly following Mr. Peterson on late-night trips to the Golden Apple Amusement Park site. For Nicky, nothing was too dangerous in pursuit of the truth.

And in turn, Nicky discovered something secret: The Neighbor was working on some terrible new machinery. Nicky needed to know what it was for. And for that, Nicky needed to enter his house.

Since nobody believes me, today I decided to break into Mr. Peterson's house.

Normally, I'd never condone breaking into someone's house. I mean, I'd be pretty mad if someone broke into my house. But this is different. This means people's lives are at stake.

My first step was to figure more about Aunt Lisa. So while the Neighbor went for a drive this morning, I broke in. And what I found was, well . . . ugh.

The whole place smelled. And I mean bad. Have you ever brought an egg salad sandwich to school and then didn't eat it and took it home and then your lunchbox smelled really bad? Well, it smelled worse than that—like rotten meat permeated through the air, everywhere. The furniture and fixtures were cracked and worn. I got the vibe that no matter how Mr. Peterson might have tried to put on a good front for the people of Raven Brooks, up close, his life was wasting away.

I pressed on, eager to learn more . . . but then the Neighbor arrived home. I quickly hid in a closet and made my escape.

But I'll collect some more evidence soon. I'm sneaking in again ASAP.

HIDE IN CLOSETS

When the Neighbor gets near, and you can't distract him, hide in closets. Remember, you've broken in, so do NOT let him catch you!

I found this image inside Mr. P.'s house today. Maybe I don't know much about being a dad, but calling your kid a "bad omen" seems kinda nuts, right? I wonder if Mr. P. blames Aaron for the tragedy that's fallen his family. That's pretty messed up. I think it's high time I contact the authorities.

9-1-1 transcript

Raven Brooks Police Department: Hi, thanks for calling the RBPD. State your name, address of emergency location, and your emergency, please.

Nicky: Nicky Roth, 910 Friendly Court. My neighbors are missing and their dad is acting weird. There's weird stuff all over his house . . .

Raven Brooks Police Department: Your neighbors are missing? What are their names, please.

Nicky: Aaron and Mya Peterson. They've been gone about four months and—

Raven Brooks Police Department: Got it. We're on our way.

RAVEN ✪ BROOKS ✪ BANNER

Peterson Children Leave Home Under Mysterious Circumstance

No foul play? Are you kidding me? Why can no one see that he's up to something? If Aaron and Mya have any chance of surviving, I guess I'm going to have to be the one to save them.

The Raven Brooks Police Department was perplexed to discover that a pair of Raven Brooks children, siblings Aaron and Mya Peterson, have gone missing without any report made to their offices.

The siblings were last seen roughly four months ago. Their mother, Diane Peterson, perished in a car accident at that time.

"As you might imagine, this is a confusing situation for us all," said the police chief. "We aren't sure where the kids are, but as far as we can tell, no rules have been broken in our jurisdiction. All that being said, we hope for their safe return."

The missing children's father, Mr. Theodore Peterson, is of course infamous for his role in the Golden Apple Amusement Park tragedy that resulted in a seven-year-old girl's death. But in a statement to the *Banner*, Mr. Peterson said his status as the town's "black sheep" is precisely why he did not contact local police about his children.

At present, the RBPD said they have no evidence to suggest foul play on Peterson's part and will be pressing no charges.

Dig Into the Buried Secrets

When word broke that Aaron and Mya were missing, the wheels were finally in motion for justice to be served. But even with the town in his corner, Nicky Roth was still two steps behind Mr. Peterson.

In the just-released *Hello Neighbor* novel *Buried Secrets*, the prequel trilogy to the original game comes to its shocking conclusion. Even as the world seems to look beyond Friendly Court for evidence that Aaron and Mya are still alive, Nicky begins to receive cryptic messages from his best friend's supposedly abandoned bedroom window.

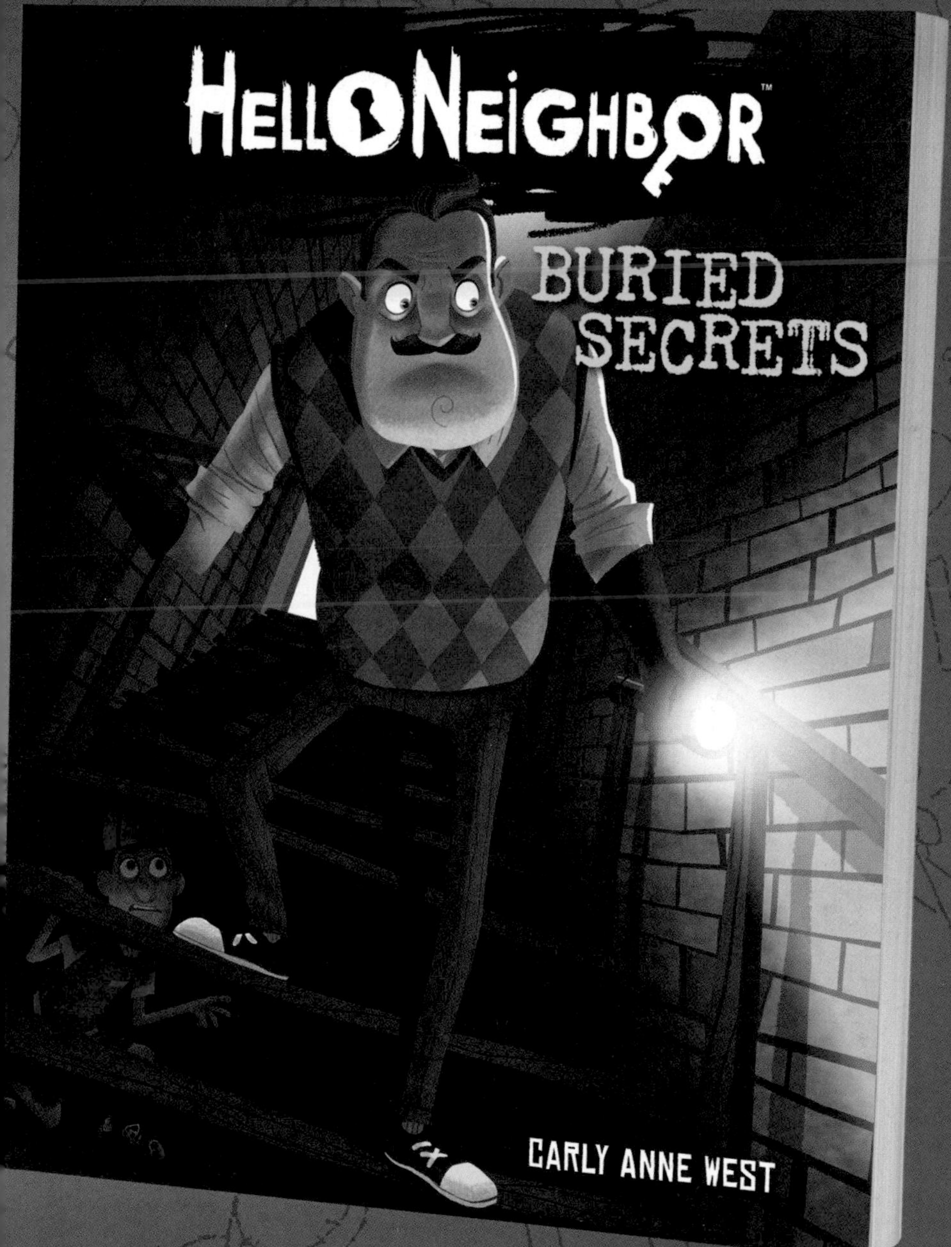
HELLO NEIGHBOR™
BURIED SECRETS
CARLY ANNE WEST

THE RAVEN BROOKS TOWN FORUM MESSAGE BOARD

Discuss your town, online!

Forum > News > People > Theodore Masters Peterson

RavenBrooksConcernedResident wrote:

Theodore Masters Peterson is no stranger 2 the news these days. We, the ppl of Raven Brooks, DESERVE ANSWERS. DO we not?!? Plz write down wat u think is happening w/ Mr. Peterson below. MayB we can come to the bottom of this case!!!!!!!Before it's 2 l8 & he takes over our town!!!!!!!!!

NeighborhoodGal101
Member since February 1995
46 posts
Has anyone else noticed the creepy mannequins that guy has? Ew.
I don't live close that man, but my dog walker does take my precious Marshmallow there from time to time. Apparently one of the mannequins came to life and jumped at her! For real!
Mr. Peterson's long been known in the town as a pariah, a creepy dude.

I think those aren't mannequins at all. See, I think those are the souls of his departed family members. And after his dearly departed wife kicked the bucket, he probably snapped and decided to preserve his family forever as faceless, legless automatons with voodoo magic.

MrPetersonTheoryDude
Member since January 1996
10 posts
For another twisted take, maybe Peterson has more than one identity. Maybe he has an Evil Twin, and actually, this is the Evil Twin. It makes sense, actually. THINK ABOUT IT. What if there are not one but TWO Mr. Petersons running around Raven Brooks?!
PS: See my other theories about Y2K in my profile!

Guest
[0 posts]
Or how about this? When we first met Mr. Peterson, he could be seen wearing shoes with the ominous number 666 on their soles. These days, he's switched up to a mysterious mark of the letter M, but is it all a coverup? Could the evil driving the Neighbor be a bit of underworld devilry so insidious that even he doesn't realize who's pulling his strings?

C-90

II

50   0

LOW NOICE

1. "There's a Creepy Neighbor Next Door"
2. "Have You Ever Really Killed a Neighbor?"
3. "I Can Hide You Like That"
4. "Unbreak My Door"
5. "Cotton Eye Nicky"
6. "Until They Sleep"
7. "Because You Hid Me"
8. "You're Making Me Alone"
9. "How Do U Do It"
10. "Killing Me Hardly With His Axe"

SIDE
1   C-90

100   50   0

Cool Songs I Wrote To Listen To While Sleuthing
Around Mr. Peterson's House   -By Enzo

S
T
E
R
E
O

Want to sleuth around
Mr. Peterson's house, too? Well,
you're in luck. You can join our
ragtag gang of kids! But first, you'll
need to play the game. You can find
more information in the next pages.
Just make sure to stay hydrated,
get your sleep, shower and bathe,
and take care of yourself, too.
If only Mya and Aaron had those
luxuries . . .

SURVIVE THE NEIGHBOR

Nicky's world is no longer just Nicky's. Now it can be yours, too—with *Hello Neighbor*.

If you're going to survive the Neighbor, you'll have to study every detail of his world. In the pages ahead, you'll find maps, hidden items, strategies, and other gameplay tips for the series' games, including an in-depth look at the game that started it all and ideas for how to team up in the new *Secret Neighbor* online game.

Just remember: Playing your way through *Hello Neighbor* won't ensure a safe ending for you—or for Nicky Roth.

In fact, it's quite the opposite.

CHAPTER 5:

Hello Neighbor Act 1

The original *Hello Neighbor* is a mind-bending horror survival adventure.

Players begin Act 1 by guiding Nicky Roth through the Neighbor's house shortly after the disappearance of Aaron and Mya Peterson.

The experience of escaping the Neighbor can be challenging. But now that you have access to what Nicky knows, you might—keyword: might—be able to live through it.

Cutscene Clues

The game opens in Nicky's point of view.

As Nicky, you see missing signs for Aaron and Mya before you hear a scream coming from the Peterson household. You don't make it to the window in time to see who's screaming, but you will see who's causing it: Mr. Peterson.

You watch Mr. Peterson lock up the unknown victim with a red key and then scope him placing the key on a table upstairs in his house.

From there, Act 1 of *Hello Neighbor* is a cat-and-mouse chase where you guide Nicky into the Neighbor's house while avoiding the Neighbor. Along the way, Nicky's first cutscene vision cracks open one of the game's biggest moments.

When it flashes to the night Mrs. Peterson died, you discover that Mr. Peterson was there when the crash happened!

That revelation is proof enough that you should stay out of the Neighbor's iron grip, but where can you hide when your goal is breaking in?

Nicky's House

This is where you'll (usually) respawn if Mr. Peterson catches you on his property. It's also your safe zone—a place where Mr. Peterson can never chase you.

Familiarize yourself with game controls by filling your inventory with items from inside the Roth house, like a pair of reading glasses and a stack of boxes in the closet that will come in handy when you try to scale the Neighbor's suburban fortress.

The Neighbor's First Floor

Rely on Nicky's map of the first floor to make it through unharmed.

Mr. P.'s tool room has everything if it can be accessed.

How do I turn this elevator on?

What's left inside is sad and broken, like the Peterson family.

Of all the creepy additions Mr. P. made to the house, this shelf may be the most useful if it can be climbed.

The staircase upstairs should be here, but it's totally walled off. Was this mystery room meant to keep me out—or to keep someone else in?

Strategies

When you're all prepped to infiltrate the Peterson household, it's time to strategize!

Did You Know?

The Neighbor is an AI, meaning the more you play, the more he learns about you and your moves. You'll want to switch it up from time to time to make sure you know just how to beat him!

Mr. Peterson always comes looking for Nicky, but the game gives you a sort of sixth sense when the villain is creeping up on you. Whenever Nicky's point of view swoons to black with a low, dreadful sound, you MUST find a hiding place or retreat to your own front porch where the Neighbor can't chase you. Otherwise, you're done for.

WHERE TO HIDE

The best hiding spots in the game are the wardrobes littered throughout the neighbor's house. To make it inside, click on the wardrobes.

Tip:

You can only hide from Mr. Peterson if he hasn't yet seen you in a room. So keep out ahead of him at all times.

ESCAPING THE NEIGHBOR

In other instances, when the Neighbor attacks, you may have to throw some of your item inventory at him to slow him down. Once you've gotten some distance, head outside and jump as high and as far as you can to get clear of his yard. Then take another crack at his house from a new angle to keep his AI programming on its toes.

Hunting the Red Key

Once you've gotten the basic moves down and explored the layout of the Peterson household, your primary Act 1 objective is to find the red key that opens the basement door.

The red key is located on a table in the bedroom of the second floor. But that's the easy part—there's no staircase on the main floor that takes you up, and the bedroom door is locked.

In order to get the red key, you will need to assemble a series of tools and tricks. Thankfully, we have tips on how to do just that!

Your real first step in getting the key is to climb your way to the second floor.

The exterior of the Peterson house is in shambles, from the jagged picket fence to the busted convertible that's been rusting on the front lawn since the accident that killed Mrs. Peterson. However, the trash that's scattered about the neighbor's house can be incredibly helpful to you. Use it well!

Start your attack by jumping up the shelf unit leaning against the left side of the front porch. From the top of this structure, you can leap to the roof on your left (you may want to bring a box up to give you a boost) and then with a running jump, travel across the ledge of the roof until you're standing in front of the two windows on the house's right side.

Make sure you have a solid item in your inventory (the trash-can lids along the street are great for this) to smash a window and arrive on the second floor.

Then, voilà! You're in!

Closed off is the upstairs bedroom. This was once a shared room for Aaron and Mya.

Once you break the window, you'll land in the room with the staircase to nowhere. While it seems the Neighbor has closed this space off from the rest of the house, there are actually secrets inside. Play with the electricity!

One of the most vital locations in Act I is the hidden room at the center of the second floor. Look for a few keys that will keep you on the path in here.

The Elevator Run

Another way to get into the bedroom is via the ramshackle elevator that the Neighbor has built on the side of his house. Seems simple enough, but in order to use it, you'll need to power up the mechanism.

Powering Up the Mechanism

1. Make sure the electrical box on the left side of the house is switched on, then climb your way up into the second floor.

2. Next, you'll need to rip a painting off the wall. This reveals a secret hole into the hidden room.

3. There you will find a large electrical switch next to the locked bedroom door. Flip the switch on to power the fan on the shelf in the main room.

4. Turn the red lever beneath the fan shelf to lift the outside elevator to the bedroom window. However, if you want to be along for the ride, you need to delay the lever's drop until you can get outside. The best way to do this involves a secret shortcut out of the staircase room.

Eagle-eyed players will note the small yellow switch located above the stairwell. Turn it to open up the first-floor access. Then you can run downstairs to get the bowling ball in the Neighbor's front room. Place the bowling ball in front of the fan and then turn its switch to blow the ball down the shelf.

It will take some timing, but eventually, you will be able to run downstairs and outside to the elevator platform before the bowling ball is blown down onto the lever. When that happens, the platform will lift you up to the key room. Just make sure you avoid the Neighbor on your run down and have something in hand to smash the bedroom window once you're lifted!

Key Method 2:
The Magnet Gun

Another way to find the red key is to obtain the magnet gun.
The magnet gun is an amazing item from the Neighbor's past. This method is less dangerous then the Elevator Run, but it is more time-consuming.

How to Get the Magnet Gun

1. Start by climbing in front of the Neighbor's house.
2. Break into the middle room via the loose painting.
3. Notice the simple door keys hanging next to the padlock? There's a key rack on the wall, too—the short key with the red handle is actually the key to Mrs. Peterson's wrecked car on the lawn.
4. Obtain the key.
5. With the new key, open the car's trunk.
6. Inside the trunk, you'll see the magnet gun, which you can obtain.

The Magnet Gun

The magnet gun is an item that will allow you to pull anything metal into your hand from a distance. **Tip:** Test it out by pulling trash cans and lids before proceeding.

How to Get the Red Key

1. Take the magnet gun behind the house.
2. Build yourself a tower of moving boxes tall enough so that you can see through the window to Mr. Peterson's workshop.
3. From here, you'll be able to collect a lockpick and a wrench.
   a. **Important:** The lockpick allows you to open most locked doors in Mr. Peterson's house (including the one to the bedroom upstairs).
   b. **Important:** The wrench will let you open the gate for the big ladder on the back of the house (which will grant you roof access to the bedroom).

Whichever path you take, you'll be able to get into the bedroom and nab the red key without the Neighbor even knowing you're in his house. Of course, once you have the red key, conflict with Mr. Peterson becomes unavoidable.

Point of No Return

Your entry into the red key's holding room will probably hit like déjà vu. That's because this is the same bedroom that Aaron and Mya started every game of hide-and-seek in. You'll notice, however, that time has treated it harshly.

For one, there's the massive hole in the ceiling. It may make entering easier, but it's also a sign that no kids have been sleeping here of late. And what purpose Mr. Peterson has for tearing apart his house is its own mystery.

But more so than the physical change, the entire bedroom is a grim monument to the lives of two kids.

But you don't have long to dawdle. With the red key in hand, it's time for you to make your fateful choice. Do you open the door to the basement solo and chase the sound of the blood-curdling screams, or do you turn back in fear?

The Neighbor's Basement

The Neighbor's basement is the largest part of the house. It's also a dark and sprawling maze. Take Nicky's survival map with you to mark your way.

In the laundry room, you'll find a washing machine. The washing machine is also a secret door. Through here, you can enter to the rest of the basement.

A broken bedroom. I can't help but think this was some incarnation of a dungeon for "bad omen" Aaron.

This power box doesn't affect the whole house, but playing with it might be the clue to escaping the basement.

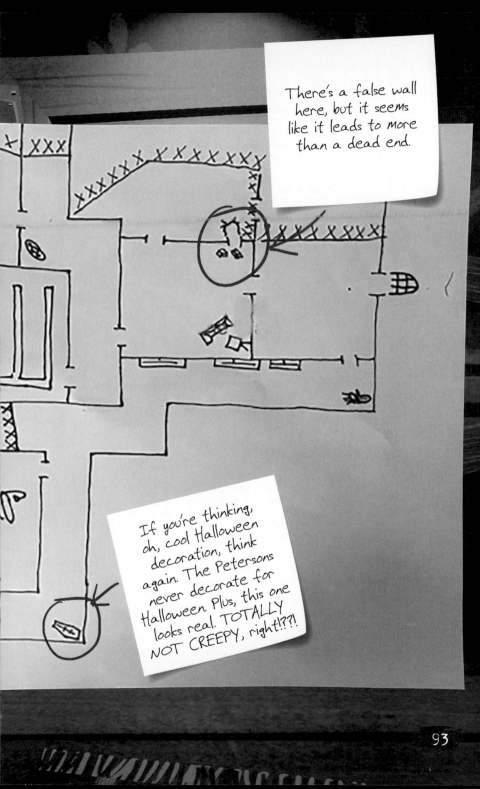

There's a false wall here, but it seems like it leads to more than a dead end.

If you're thinking, oh, cool Halloween decoration, think again. The Petersons never decorate for Halloween. Plus, this one looks real. TOTALLY NOT CREEPY, right!???!

The Laundry Room & Secret Entrance

Laundry rooms might typically be for cleaning, but not in Mr. Peterson's house.

Like most of what you'll see in the finale of Act 1, this room is merely an obstacle.

1. Start by opening the washing machine itself. The front of the unit is actually a secret door that leads into the rest of the basement system. Strike right through the first small room and through its standard door into the green bedroom. That's where the nature of this level really takes shape.

Scan around the bedroom and you'll see: The bed is little more than a pallet, and all around the ground are strewn cans, candles, and a basketball. This was likely where Aaron was kept in a holding space.

In this room, your goal is escape. To do so:

1. Take a can or any item you don't need.

2. Smash out one of the windows in the room (we recommend one on the side of the room with two windows).

3. Jump out.

What you'll find next is, well . . .

Discover the Dark

After jumping through the broken window, you'll find a major power switch to your left. You'll want to keep track of this—make a mental note of its location for later in the level.

Turn to your right to spot a small lever on the wall. Flip this, and you'll see the metal gate that separates you from the rest of the basement rise. Walk across.

When you've passed the gate, you'll be able to access a number of rooms that were previously blocked.

Tip:

Spend a little time breaking down these items that block your way (i.e. chairs) to make your journey through the dark halls easier.

Always keep in mind: Mr. Peterson is still lurking somewhere nearby, so having objects to throw at him and escape routes open are both essential for your survival.

Your main objective at this point is to find an area lit by a red light bulb. Once there, you'll see the very first (and thankfully inert) mannequin you'll encounter in this game. There's a flashlight nearby, which will be helpful to navigate the darker parts of the basement, but what you want to do is pull the lever next to the mannequin.

The Generator Gambit

The room beyond the mannequin has a door that looks like it may be your way back out. However, that door itself is blocked by a metal gate.

You'll need to access the generator instead, which lies on the other side of the fence.

In order to gain access to the generator, go out the door to your left and look along the wall in the next room. You'll find a dark spot in the brickwork. Toss any solid object at this spot to topple the bricks and create a secret passage.

Tips:

- Keep your flashlight with you! This will help you navigate better.
- Open blocked doors. This will clear your path for later.

Of course, there are still obstacles in your way—like an electric fence!

- To avoid electroshock, return to the main power switch near the bedroom and turn it off. This will re-lock some of the levered doors you initially went through, but you should have a new path of doors that you already opened.

Once you've turned the generator's light from red to green, the switch that controls the escape door will be fully operational.

Dead-End Dad

Unfortunately, once you've "escaped" the confines of the basement via the door, you'll find there actually is no escape.

What you'll find instead is a dead-end tunnel built of rickety boards. Its end is a door locked three times over. Inevitably, at this stage, the Neighbor will catch you.

MISSING

Name: Nicholas Roth
Age: Thirteen
Last seen: Playing in his yard

Young Nicholas "Nicky" Roth is a good kid with no known reasons to run away. Raven Brooks police are operating under the assumption that the boy's disappearance is a kidnapping. If you see this child, please call authorities. Reward being offered by the Roth family for any news leading to his safe return.

CHAPTER 6:
Secret Neighbor Guide

Once you complete the first act of *Hello Neighbor*, you'll realize that as Nicky Roth, you're trapped in the Neighbor's basement for the long haul.

But what about Raven Brooks? Did the town ignore the disappearance of another local kid? Did Nicky's parents suspect that Mr. Peterson was at fault?

One crew of intrepid kids knew what Nicky knew. One group of friends was the last line of defense against Mr. Peterson. And their story rolls out in the action of *Secret Neighbor*.

Secret Neighbor allows you to explore Mr. Peterson's house along with your online friends or a new group of fans. What's most important here is that you work together, because you're not just escaping a computer Neighbor this time—you're facing off against a real human being.

The story of Nicky's friends and their quest to save him from Mr. Peterson's basement begins after his disappearance. In that time, the landscape of the house has changed dramatically, so there are plenty of new corners to explore as you try and unlock a much more complex basement door.

Read on for the inside scoop on how *Secret Neighbor* puts your team to the ultimate survival test.

Who Is the Neighbor Now?

In *Secret Neighbor*, you'll assume the role of one of four kids making a run at the Peterson house to save Nicky Roth. Or at least it'll look that way. In truth, one of the players is actually Mr. Peterson himself. That means there's a twenty-five percent chance you'll become the villain of your own game!

As the Neighbor, it'll be your job to deceive the other players and pick them off one by one. While chasing them down and grabbing them is always a classic option, the multiplayer format allows for more creative ways for the action to unfold.

For one, the Neighbor now has the uncanny ability to appear as a neighborhood child. That means the others won't know who the secret villain of the game is until the Neighbor reveals themselves. Additionally, if the player who serves as Mr. Peterson equips themselves with a mask, they can take on the look and screenname of another gamer to truly boggle the minds of the others.

Another item that plays into this version is the kid-detecting sonar device that the Neighbor player can discover in the house. This equips the player with the ability to see all the kids no matter where they are. Across floors and through walls, no one can escape Mr. Peterson for long—especially when he's dropping bear traps to hold you in place before you find Nicky.

Ironically, the hidden adversary aspect of the game means that the only way you will survive is by trusting your teammates to help you. But in the end, you can really trust no one but yourself.

Still, there's hope for the other players yet. And once you know the personalities of the characters you'll be becoming, you'll know you have a fighting chance.

The Secret Infiltrators

Though readers met them initially in the *Hello Neighbor* novels, the trio of Nicky's friends who organized the kid army to infiltrate the Neighbor's house become their own heroes over the course of *Secret Neighbor*. Each of them has their own reason for wanting to save Nicky or at least take the fight to Mr. Peterson, and each of them has the capability to save the day when the moment of truth arises.

Enzo Esposito

Enzo is Nicky's best friend in Raven Brooks. He's a fast-talking, quick-thinking athlete. While the pair met through their lifelong pal dads, their own friendship was fast and unique. Enzo is a championship gamer, a basketball showboat, and an opinionated adventurer. While he and Nicky seem different on the surface, they share a sense of sarcastic humor.

When Nicky made it clear that he wanted to go after Mr. Peterson, Enzo was reluctant to attack without evidence. But since Nicky disappeared into the depths of the Neighbor's house, Enzo has become as dedicated to getting his friend out as Nicky was to saving Aaron. Now Enzo wears the unlikely mantle of field team leader, though he knows he'd be nowhere without some familiar teammates.

Maritza Esposito

Though the youngest of the infiltrating crew, Maritza has the deepest personal connection to the Peterson story. As the third member of the original Golden Apple Young Inventors Club, she watched as first her pal Lucy Yi and then presumably her bestie Mya Peterson were destroyed by the insanity of the Neighbor.

Despite her tragic part as the last survivor of this friend circle, Maritza remains an optimist in the face of Mr. Peterson's strange evil. She knows that there are terrible things in this world, but she chooses to fight back with the hope that justice can be served.

Trinity Bales

The analytical nerve center of the operation, Trinity brings more to the table than her encyclopedic knowledge of Raven Brooks and her top-notch oboe-playing skills. She was the first person with no direct connection to the Peterson case to believe Nicky, and when she saw the evil that lurked in Mr. Peterson's home she committed to the cause hard.

Trinity always has a sharp scheme or two for staying out of the Neighbor's way or finding the perfect method for uncovering a hidden secret. With her on the team, the infiltrating squad will likely always be one step ahead of the Neighbor, but should Trinity get caught, can the rest of the kids in the crew solider on without her?

Behind the Neighbor's Walls

One of the first things you'll notice in *Secret Neighbor* is how much Mr. Peterson's house has changed even in the short period since Nicky went missing after Act 1 of the original game.

For example, the Neighbor erected tall fencing all around his yard to keep snooping kids out and keep his sinister plans for his prisoners inside.

The house has many more stories than it did previously, almost as if it's growing into some sort of tower. Players will discover all-new locales like the Neighbor's gnarly garage, double staircase, his sickening shed, and a foggy greenhouse.

And if you're seeing the game from Mr. Peterson's perspective? You'll also get access to his security-centered CCTV Room where he spies on every wicked inch he's built on the house.

The Key to Success

In *Secret Neighbor*, as a team, you're looking for five keys to unlock the basement door. The multiplayer format turns your hunt into a timed event that makes speed and wits more important than ever.

In order to stay one step ahead of the secret Neighbor in your midst, coordination is key.

Tips:

- Try talking to your teammates and send everyone to a different floor of the house to rifle through cabinets and overturn furniture. Each key you want to find is color-coordinated with a lock on the basement door, and some of them will turn up in the most unexpected of places.

- Ask yourself: Did you open every cabinet in the greenhouse? Do you empty every stray desk? Did you scan the highest shelf in every closet?

As you make your frenzied search, the Neighbor will be trying to sneak up on you. If they catch you, you'll see footage where Mr. Peterson adds your character's photo to his catalog of victims.

The lucky twist is that unlike Nicky Roth, you now have a chance to wriggle your way out of the Neighbor's clutches. If you're the Neighbor, know that you're not invincible. If you're a kid, remember that you can fight your way out of Peterson's grip . . . but you have to act fast!

test-sn35lounge.tinybuild.com

CHAPTER 7:
Hello Neighbor Act 2

After being captured by the Neighbor, Nicky Roth isn't sure how much time has passed. Has it been weeks? Months? Years? Nicky can't quite tell. Worse yet, if he doesn't get out soon, he'll probably lose his mind, too.

This is the crux of *Hello Neighbor* Act 2. Nicky once was so desperate to get into Mr. Peterson's house—now he'd do anything to never see it again.

To escape, you'll need to carefully break past the house's defenses. And along the way, you'll uncover the last pieces of concrete evidence we have about Mrs. Peterson's, Aaron's, and Mya's final fates.

This Is Now

When you awake back in Nicky's shoes, you find yourself in a much more lived-in version of the faux bedroom at the heart of the Neighbor's basement. Whether it once belonged to Aaron or not, it's been yours for a long time by the look of it.

Some of the biggest unanswered questions in all of *Hello Neighbor* come from this missing time period. How long was Nicky in the house for? Did he ever find proof that Aaron or Mya lived?

What you know for sure is that Nicky has changed in intervening time between acts. His legs have sprouted, and his clothes are an ill-fitting mess. You look at his hands only to see bandages and at his feet to see a shoe missing. Regardless of whether this body is ready, it's now or never.

Stalk the Yard

Spy through the keyhole to set off the chain of events that will lead to your release. After you hear an object fall over, try the door again. You'll find that a mysterious force has unlocked the door. Could it be Aaron, or is it a phantom of this haunted house?

Once you're outside the bedroom, head for the glowing air-conditioning vent. Remove the grate and crawl your way into the ducts that make up the veins of the Peterson house.

The air ducts lead you out of the basement and to the sweet, free air of your neighborhood for the first time in what's probably been forever. But that freedom isn't quite at hand yet.

The backyard Nicky discovers is far different from the one he entered when the game began. Now the fences seen in *Secret Neighbor* taunt you with their overpowering, insurmountable height. What's more, the exterior of building has been fitted with a series of scaffold-like pipes and fixtures. It's clear that the entire system helps the Neighbor keep your basement prison closed to the outside world. In order to escape, you must break it all apart.

The attack-on-the-pipes method of escaping the Neighbor's house requires a two-step procedure. First, you have to open the system up to flush it out, and next you've got to turn it to your advantage by flooding aspects of the property with a special wheel you'll pick up along the way.

To start your mission, look for the gauge that monitors the pipe system in the backyard. Getting its needle to redline is step one in breaking the Neighbor's control.

Flipping Out

In order to flip the gauge's needle to red, you'll have to turn a trio of levers located on pipes around the property.

1. The first is situated down the security fence from the gauge, an easy pull to get the plan rolling.

2. The second lever you'll notice sits high up in the air on the long pipe that connects the lawn and the house. Reaching that height requires a tool you're well acquainted with from Act 1—the wrench. This means that if you want to truly escape the property, you have to go back to the last place Nicky ever wants to go: inside Mr. Peterson's house.

Break a window and reenter the first floor as fast as you can to avoid the Neighbor. You'll find your tool in the kitchen freezer. Grab it and swiftly head back to the yard.

Once the wrench is in hand, you'll want to unscrew the fence that protects the house's exterior ladder. Climbing the ladder will show you just how tall the Neighbor's tower of terror has grown, so be careful not to fall off the roof before you reach your goal. Follow the line of pipes to the place you saw the lever from the ground, and again employ your wrench to loosen it up for a full hand turn.

While that high-wire adventure makes Nicky anxious enough, the next leg draws the Neighbor even nearer.

Return to
the Scene of the Crime

The third and final lever is in the heart of Mr. Peterson's house, right off the main entrance.

Locate a blue lever near the sofa. Pull it, then take it back to the yard. From there, you need to slink your way to one last impenetrable part of Mr. Peterson's house.

In the tight outside corner where three windows meet, break the one that stands on its own. This should lead you to the cramped junk room that leads to the boiler room. Turning this on will unleash pressure through the pipe system you've been opening up.

Back where you began, you'll find that not only has the pressure gauge maxed out but that the pipe's main valve wheel has busted loose, pouring sticky sewage everywhere. Far from being an accident, this is just what you wanted.

Take the red wheel. Keep it safe—it's the most important tool you'll use for the entire act.

Make It Rain

There are several locations around the house where you can employ the red wheel to open valves in the massive plumbing system. Each of these open valves create their own chain reaction that will alter the landscape of the Neighbor's house.

Spend some time testing out as many different valves as you can. Each of these locations is a spot on a pipe that is marked by red bands, though you'll have to fit the wheel to the bolt in order to make it flow.

Pipes you can test:

- On the roof
- Inside the Neighbor's house
- Tucked away in odd corners and rooms

For now, focus your efforts on draining the water from the Neighbor's indoor pool. But beware—there's some beasts called "Sharkotrons" in this room, too. These toys, once popular with Raven Brooks kids, have been transformed into lethal eating machines by the Neighbor. Defeat them by draining their habitat out onto the lawn.

Good news. Once you do that, there's an item at the bottom of the pool that's pivotal to the rest of the game: Mr. Peterson's shovel.

Secret Scenes, Final Visions

In one scene, we finally witness the loss of Mrs. Peterson. Nicky looks on at an empty hospital bed whose heart monitor is fading out. Around the corner, Mr. Peterson paces as a wrecked man—the Neighbor holding on to his last shred of hope and sanity. A moment later, Mrs. Peterson is gone.

Later in the act, you'll flash to a topsy-turvy version of the Rotten Core roller coaster.

In this final dive into the tragedy of the Petersons, you do more than relive a sad memory. You're taking on a ride through the stomach-turning fun house that was their lives as the family fell apart.

As you return to the world of the game, you'll begin to see some concrete answers for what happened in the house before Nicky was captured.

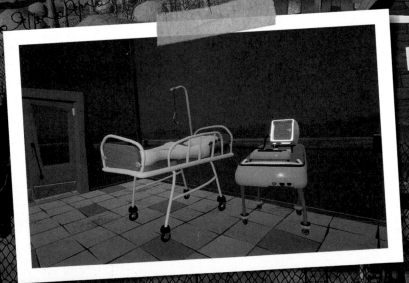

Digging Up the Dollhouse

As the final big challenge of Act 2, you dig up what Mr. Peterson has buried in the ground.

Once you have the Neighbor's shovel from upstairs, dig in the backyard where the grass turns to dirt.

From there, you'll find an empty coffin.

Or more accurately, a mostly empty coffin. At the bottom is a single key tied with a pink ribbon. Take that key back into the house where a battered version of Aaron and Mya's room still exists. The key will open the door to Mya's dollhouse—an object that itself moans and moves in accordance with whatever happens.

By opening the dollhouse completely, you'll open up the last remaining areas of the real house. Most important, it opens a door around the corner containing a yellow control box. That's all vital for one final run at grabbing your best escape tool.

Frozen Finale vs. Crowbar Climax

There are three paths to the last major reveal of Act 2, and all of them take a lot of small detail work.

Option One

The first way involves reversing the work you did on certain valves in order to reflood the highest levels of the house. Check the valve that hangs above the back lawn on a system of pipes. And the one near the spigot spitting water onto the lawn. And the one right next to the boiler where you started your whole water-pumping journey. Then finally the valve on the top floor near the spigot in the top-floor room full of radiators.

If you can get those pipes turned your way, it should start to flood cold water back into Mr. Peterson's house and specifically to that radiator room spigot. This is the moment made for the yellow control box that the dollhouse opened for you. Throw that switch and watch as the water in the radiator room freezes over like a pond in winter. With that task done, you'll be able to slide across the ice into the highest and final room in the Neighbor's house. That's where the final red key is located to open the door to the fence in the front yard!

Option Two

Of course, if you're in the mood for a creepier path to freedom, you can head to the bathroom downstairs. There you will find a curious item: a toy construction man carrying an inaccessible crowbar. If you pick this toy up and roll back upstairs to the dollhouse, you can sit the man on the toilet in the dollhouse itself.

Placing the toy there will cause another large toy man to reappear in the first-floor bathroom, only this time he'll let you take the crowbar from him! With that handy tool in your grasp, head straight to the part of the fence that looks like it's held together by loosely-nailed boards. The crowbar will pull these boards off the fence and lead the player out onto the street!

The Trampoline Gambit

One alternate and simplified method for escaping the Neighbor's fenced-in fortress in Act 2 is to bounce your way out. But simple in theory does not mean quick in practice.

For the players who are most nimble with their controls and patient with their gameplay, you can bounce your way out of the yard using the still-fenced trampoline. Part of its protective barrier can be knocked down when you empty the pool room's water, but no matter what, you can jump to this tramp with practice.

Like the rest of the yard, the tramp is surrounded by an unclimbable fence, which makes it virtually invisible from the ground. Only if you swipe the wrench as you did before to gain roof access can you even peer at the elastic means of escape. And just being on the roof is not nearly high enough to jump over the trampoline's fence.

In order to make this escape happen, you'll need to bring a number of boxes up onto the roof from the yard. Stacking them on the outcropping near the trampoline is a difficult test of your patience and skill. And once you get enough height to make a leap of faith, you still don't go straight to the tramp.

Shoot to clear or land on the small ledge along the trampoline fence, so long as you get over and onto the target-painted tramp in the end. Then it may still take a few jumps to build up enough air to finally escape the yard—all while the Neighbor rages at you from his lawn. So prepare for the ultimate test of your abilities if you want to say you flew to freedom.

Farewell for Now

While Mr. Peterson wants to hunt you down, a last terrified scream calls out from his house. What was it?

Nicky escapes the Neighbor, but can he ever really escape what happened to him?

To find the answers, we have to flash-forward years in the story to a time that's somehow more desperate and deadly than the one we've already experienced.

CHAPTER 8:
Hello Neighbor Act 3

The most dramatic transformation in all of *Hello Neighbor* isn't Mr. Peterson's descent into madness, nor is it the wild growth of his deadly house.

No. In truth, the weirdest evolution of the entire saga is Nicky Roth's transition from kid to adult.

Physically, Nicky may look like his old self with a few more feet in height and a little more stubble on the chin. But when you look at his eyes, a weariness creeps around the edges. In truth, Nicky could never really grow up. He could never really get past the trauma of Mr. Peterson. And even as he tries to go on ahead with his life, something still draws him back to a war he thought he'd escaped long ago.

This stressful existence is the backbone of *Hello Neighbor*'s final act.

Steel yourself for one final descent. Cross the fence. Climb into the basement. Seek out threats both living and undead as you attempt to change Nicky's fate in the final battle with the Neighbor.

Days Gone By

When we pick back up with Nicky Roth, everything about his life has changed. Years have passed since his time in captivity with Mr. Peterson. Nicky now lives in his own apartment. But something still haunts him from his youth. And that's what (along with an eviction notice) brings Nicky back to Raven Brooks.

After years of tragedy and cover-ups, the little town has finally succumbed to a cruel fate. Once-shining parts of the community have become destroyed, and at the heart of the rot is one ruined property: Mr. Peterson's house. Now a pile of charred walls and broken memories, the home looks almost harmless.

As he walks the streets, Nicky is haunted by a shadowy Thing—a supernatural beast. Nicky then takes the key to Mr. Peterson's from his car trunk, and discovers that the phone at the Neighbor's is still connected.

Nicky has an evil feeling. He takes a nap and tries to shrug the feeling off, but that's right when his final adventure begins.

Night Moves

As before, it all starts with a scream.

Act 3 picks up at an undetermined moment in the game's timeline. As you peer out the window, lights shine from the Peterson house. Mr. Peterson is obviously up to his old tricks.

Your primary goal early in the act is simply to gain access to this new house and its intense roller-coaster construction. To start this journey, you'll need to turn the red lever above a door that's visible through the window on the right side of the house. Take a box with you to get that high and then pull it down without entering.

Continue through the dark by running around to the back of the house. You'll see Mr. Peterson struggling to keep someone (or something) at bay, but keep moving past the scene to a window where the white lamp shines. Break it and enter, then climb the ladder you find all the way up to the top floor. From there, you will barely be able to make out a square skylight window below you. Jump down and through that where you'll land on the tracks of the house.

Walk along the track until you reach the control room, and then carefully flip the switch on the left side of the panel followed by pushing the red button. This will start up the coaster. Avoid the roller-coaster carts for now. You goal isn't to ride the machine but to prepare to control it later on.

From there, drop through the hole in the floor and land on the lawn. Your best bet here is to let Mr. Peterson catch you, because for what comes next, you'll want daylight on your side.

Get Equipped

You wake up back in your house, ready to take the fight to the Neighbor one more time. The big goal here is to reassemble your escape kit including the red key, a crowbar, and an umbrella. Once you have everything you need, you'll force your way back into the basement for the final battle.

Enter through the front door, then make a right to a staircase at whose top is blocked by a jail cell-like cage. You can get past this by jumping from the light in the wall and over the cage. Inside the room, knock down as many Golden Apple paintings as you can until one opens a secret passage through the big Golden Apple portrait. Pull the lever to lift the gate and go back to where the painting passage is.

Run up the winding staircase revealed by your actions until you spot the room with the red-and-white stripes around the door. In there, you'll find a lever that is in a red box on the wall protected by a grate. The trick here is to grab the shoe off the shelf and throw it through the grate to turn the lever. This will open the other red box connected by a long black cord. Once opened, you'll have the red key again.

For your last items, you'll need to go back out, through the room with the box of basketballs and open the door blocked by a chair. In there, you'll see the crowbar hidden in the electrical box, but you won't be able to grab it yet. It's too hot! Let it drop through the floor to the room below and then drop down yourself and retrieve the umbrella from that room. Drop down through another hole and in the room below, you'll find the magnet gun again on the bottom of the purple shelf.

Take this back upstairs, and once you've secured the hot crowbar with the magnet gun, take it to the lower-floor bathroom and cool the bar down with the water. After this, there's only one more critical item but it will have to wait until you've conquered your greatest fears.

The Roller-Coaster Run

To fully master *Hello Neighbor*, you can't just rush into the basement like you did in Act 1. So for this second shot at disrupting Mr. Peterson's plans, you'll need to level up with some hidden achievements. And the path to your training begins by mastering the roller-coaster apparatus that brought so much anguish to Raven Brooks.

Return to the tall ladder in the back that takes you to the roller-coaster control room. Be sure to keep your umbrella with you at all times. Once you're up high, you'll want it to slow your plummeting in case you fall off the house. At first, you can ride the cart along until you reach its next room, but then you'll jump out and turn the lever to slow the cart to a stop just outside the room. If you've timed it right, the cart will be sitting next to a big section of pipe. Toss a box on the tracks so you can leap from box to pipe to cart roof from which you can ascend to the highest levels of the house.

One location you want to land at with your umbrella is the bizarre orchard that Mr. Peterson has grown at the apex of the main house. Among the trees, you'll find a mechanical box protecting a series of gears. Throw a box in there to bring the electromagnet in the coaster control room to a halt. This will allow you to pick up the green key, which is useful later.

Face Your Fears

You'll need to unlock new abilities by facing down three "Fear Rooms" whose mini adventures power you up with all-new Neighbor-avoiding abilities. Each of these levels-within-the game represent a different fearsome scenario Mr. Peterson has built to both captivate and crush the spirit of kids like Nicky, so expect terror around every corner.

The challenge of the Fear Rooms begins when you make a mad leap from the orchard and toward the small single room that stands on stilts high in the sky. Once you've dropped in through the skylight, you'll find a door that can only be opened with the red key. This lands you inside a nightmarish realm of the Fear Darkness room.

The rooftop Fear Darkness room is your last time running through a massive, twisted version of the Neighbor's world that's just beyond our reality. This time, Nicky plays the role of Tom Thumb as everything is massive in a room where darkness creeps in to swallow you at every turn and spectral whispers fill your ears with haunting accusations.

Use the room to your advantage. Bounce off the toaster springs. Topple boards to create a path up the wall. Toss darts into the wood to build your own bridge up the wall. Slowly but surely, you'll be able to follow the green arrows toward a pull chain in the ceiling that will light up a new view of the world. Getting that chain pulled both gets you out of the room and earns you the ability to double jump—leaping higher in the house than ever before.

Next on your run of achievement-unlocking hits is the dreaded Fear Supermarket. Gain access to this room by getting the blue key in the second-floor room with no floor. Remove the Golden Apple painting and nab the key with your magnet gun. Once in hand, head to the third floor and open the blue padlocked door, then use the lever to lift yourself up and into the Fear Room.

At long last, Nicky faces down the living mannequins that have haunted his dreams in a strange supermarket. The key here is to crouch down to avoid the slivered hands of the enemy while also watching to see what they're shopping for. If you can find all five items that the mannequins are hoarding and place them in your own cart without being caught, you'll gain the ability to become invisible and avoid Mr. Peterson like never before.

Finish your power-up Fear Room run with a harsh lesson from the Fear School. This room is located centrally on the first floor of the house, near the stairs and hidden behind some boxes. Unlock it with the green key you picked up after breaking the electromagnet in the control room, and you're ready to enroll in the last educational institute you'll need to survive.

Fear School is essentially a long obstacle course where Nicky has to duck and dodge his way through the longest school day of his life. Everywhere you turn, hyper-fast mannequin students clog the path. But you can avoid them by stuffing yourself into lockers. The real challenge is avoiding the white-hot teacher mannequin—especially when it rings the bell that brings its automaton student body to order. Hold fast in a locker until movement picks up again and then run on through to face one final physical threat. But by then, you'll have gained the ability to push off the mannequins advances—an ability that will stick with you when you return to the Neighbor's world.

Back to the Basement

It's happening again. Once more, Nicky Roth must descend into Mr. Peterson's underworld, but this time, Nicky is an expert.

Your last step in the house is getting the basement key card out of the freezer on the first floor. Doing this is a two-step process where you must bust the generator that powers the freezer first and then pull the key card out to let it thaw.

Run down the tracks to the left side of the house until you see the generator inside a small wire box. Use the umbrella to leap into the window above it and gather all the items you can find in this section of the house, like a guitar, a toy truck, a hat, and a flashlight. You must arrange these items on the series of shelves so they match the picture on the opposite wall. Once the shelves have been put back in order, the fencing around the generator will open and allow you to turn it off.

Then head to the kitchen and pull the key card out while avoiding Mr. Peterson at his most vengeful. It's a tight run, but with your achievement powers, you should be able to get the card in hand. Take it and the crowbar to the basement door to open that horrifying portal one final time.

Rush through the basement the way you did before. Laundry room to dark maze, straight to the back to the false brick wall. Use your new double-jump abilities to launch over the fence that stands between you and the white door. And then finally, follow the narrow hallway toward the escape that eluded you in Act 2.

Strike from the High Ground

It appears that Nicky Roth's persistence did more than expose the Neighbor. It's made him turn to the supernatural.

Nicky discovers that beyond a cardboard cutout, there's no sign of Aaron or anyone that the Neighbor has been keeping hidden. Instead, there's a GIGANTIC Mr. Peterson waiting for you.

Utilize the same giant items you've seen through the franchise to bring this goal closer to you. Start by throwing boxes in order to flip the light switch up the green wall and then head toward the radio so you can launch yourself off the toaster springs and onto the green platforms above. Throwing a second switch up top will raise the circular wooden platform. This makeshift elevator lifts you through a massive glass tube and to another room that's your size. Break in and flip the switch there, but that will just drop you to the ground again, so grab one of the many umbrellas as they fall with you.

With the umbrella, you'll have the control to launch and float yourself into the red-and-black lodge that stands off the ground. In there, you can steal a candle from the birthday cake, which can set off the fireworks by the Neighbor's feet.

Other weapons present themselves as you jump the various heights including the golf balls, which make him stumble once they're pushed down the funnel and a bow-and-dart, which incapacitates him further. If you strike the Neighbor enough times, he'll collapse to his knees, and you can launch yourself into his back house and your final confrontation.

Haunted by the Thing

Once you're deep inside, there are no more mysteries to solve. Just ones to witness.

In the midst of this broken psychic household, you'll find yourself, or at least the younger version of Nicky Roth. A stand-in for all the wayward kids who have crossed Mr. Peterson, this Nicky has no goal but to run from the epic Thing that prowls outside the window.

This Thing is the full-blown form of the monster that's been haunting Raven Brooks and Nicky's own memories for years. Whether it was the cause of Mr. Peterson's madness or something born from his black soul, the Thing seems all-powerful in a tantrum that shatters room after room of this flimsy house. Follow your young Nicky counterpart to see the pure fury of the villain, but all you can really do is survive.

Then the dust clears, all that's left is the pure void and one final house. This small, dilapidated structure is the final resting pace of Mr. Peterson. In the end, the Neighbor could never really escape the horrors he unleashed on his own family, and so it's his fate to "live" with what he did in a house alone for eternity.

Sweet Escape

If you're skilled enough to make it all the way through *Hello Neighbor*, you'll at last be rewarded with a happy ending. Or at least as close to happy as Nicky Roth can find.

Whether Nicky's final run against Mr. Peterson took place or whether it was all in his mind, no one can say. But as he wakes up the morning after that night when the phone call and the Thing haunted him, our hero seems finally unburdened by his past.

In the light of day, the remains of the Peterson household no longer look evil. Instead, they're just some old burnt boards waiting to be swept away so Raven Brooks can be rebuilt. And Nicky will be rebuilding, too. While his boyhood home is a shambles after years of abuse, he's ready to settle back here full-time and put both the house and himself together.

Sometimes, we find peace. Nicky Roth is proof that anything is possible.

But what really became of Mr. Peterson and his family? Well, no one knows for certain, but the future of the *Hello Neighbor* franchise is being written right now . . . by you.

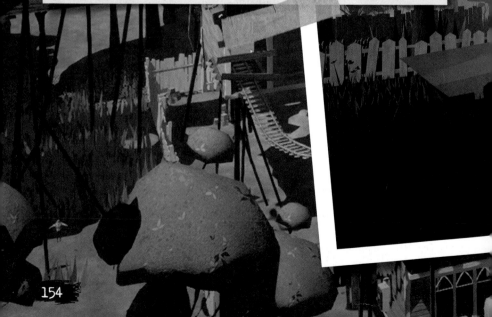

Your Next Challenge:
Become the Neighbor

Nicky Roth's story may have concluded, but the teams at Dynamic Pixels and tinyBuild are hard at work delivering future installment of *Hello Neighbor* to terrify and challenge you.

The next new game is a dynamic constructor game where you put yourself in the mind of Mr. Peterson and build all-new levels to trap and train others for survival. And here we have an exclusive first look at the tools of the trade you can utilize in your own quest to make an unbeatable house.

Will your neighborhood home be built in a vast wilderness or an endless suburban nightmare? What kinds of machines be they amusement rides or electric shockers will populate the floors? Can you create a level whose secrets are hidden, hinted at, and ultimately horrifying?

More snapshots from the world of *Hello Neighbor*

HELLONEIGHBOR™

The End??

After playing your way through the entire franchise, there is still more story to explore with *Hello Neighbor*.

First of all, what truly happened to Aaron Peterson? It seems clear that Nicky's lost friend was trapped by his father. But was Aaron truly the Bad Omen his dad always feared he was? And did he make it out?

Moreover, what happened to Nicky? After he escaped the Neighbor's house, did his investigation end? Was his reappearance a galvanizing experience for Raven Brooks, or did Mr. Peterson escape blame once again? And when exactly did Act 3 take place in Nicky's life, if at all?

Whatever the answers, in the world of *Hello Neighbor*, there's no true escape from evil. There is no final goodbye.